# Dear Parents:

Congratulations! Your child is taking the first steps on an exciting journey. The destination? Independent reading!

**STEP INTO READING®** will help your child get there. The program offers five steps to reading success. Each step includes fun stories and colorful art or photographs. In addition to original fiction and books with favorite characters, there are Step into Reading Non-Fiction Readers, Phonics Readers and Boxed Sets, Sticker Readers, and Comic Readers—a complete literacy program with something to interest every child.

## Learning to Read, Step by Step!

**Ready to Read   Preschool–Kindergarten**
• big type and easy words • rhyme and rhythm • picture clues
For children who know the alphabet and are eager to begin reading.

**Reading with Help   Preschool–Grade 1**
• basic vocabulary • short sentences • simple stories
For children who recognize familiar words and sound out new words with help.

**Reading on Your Own   Grades 1–3**
• engaging characters • easy-to-follow plots • popular topics
For children who are ready to read on their own.

**Reading Paragraphs   Grades 2–3**
• challenging vocabulary • short paragraphs • exciting stories
For newly independent readers who read simple sentences with confidence.

**Ready for Chapters   Grades 2–4**
• chapters • longer paragraphs • full-color art
For children who want to take the plunge into chapter books but still like colorful pictures.

**STEP INTO READING®** is designed to give every child a successful reading experience. The grade levels are only guides; children will progress through the steps at their own speed, developing confidence in their reading. The F&P Text Level on the back cover serves as another tool to help you choose the right book for your child.

Remember, a lifetime love of reading starts with a single step!

*To Madi*
*—C.R.*

Text copyright © 2023 by Candice Ransom
Cover art and interior illustrations copyright © 2023 by Ashley Evans

Visit us on the Web!
StepIntoReading.com
rhcbooks.com

Educators and librarians, for a variety of teaching tools, visit us at RHTeachersLibrarians.com

*Library of Congress Cataloging-in-Publication Data*
Names: Ransom, Candice F., author. | Evans, Ashley, illustrator.
Title: Graduation day! / by Candice Ransom ; illustrated by Ashley Evans.
Description: First edition. | New York : Random House Children's Books, [2023] | Series: Step into reading | Audience: Ages 4–6. | Summary: Brother prepares for his graduation day using all of the skills he has learned throughout the year.
Identifiers: LCCN 2022022907 (print) | LCCN 2022022908 (ebook) |
ISBN 978-0-593-64364-8 (trade paperback) | ISBN 978-0-593-64365-5 (library binding) |
ISBN 978-0-593-64366-2 (ebook)
Subjects: CYAC: Stories in rhyme. | Graduation (School)—Fiction. | LCGFT: Stories in rhyme. | Picture books.
Classification: LCC PZ8.3.R1467 Gp 2023 (print) | LCC PZ8.3.R1467 (ebook) | DDC [E]—dc23

Printed in the United States of America
10 9 8 7 6 5 4 3 2 1
First Edition

This book has been officially leveled by using the F&P Text Level Gradient™ Leveling System.

STEP INTO READING®

STEP 1 READY TO READ

# Graduation Day!

by Candice Ransom
illustrated by Ashley Evans

Random House New York

Almost ready.
Can not be late.
Today is the day
I graduate!

Big sis helps me
tie my shoes.

Race to the bus.

I win! You lose!

Teacher greets us
with a hug.

8

We sit on the
story rug.

Morning song
sung one last time.

Hurry! Grab the
tub of slime!

# Pencil helper.

# Lead the line.

# Classroom jobs
# that have been mine!

On my worksheet—
three gold stars!

Now I can go
play with cars.

Learn a new word.

Copy letters.

Hand writing is

getting better!

Counting, writing,

I can do.

But I can not
tie my shoe.

# Clean out cubby.

Walk down hall.
Take my picture
off the wall.

Caps and gowns
for all ten.

Shoelace loose!

Try again.

Dance and sing.

Clap, clap, clap.

Wave our hands.

Bump my cap!

One more try to

tie my shoe.

Did you see what
I can do?

Goodbye, cubby.

Goodbye, hall.

Goodbye, classrooms,
till next fall!

# Goodbye, teachers!
# Everyone!

Next year, first grade.

Here I come!

*For Anne Temme*
*—J. H.*

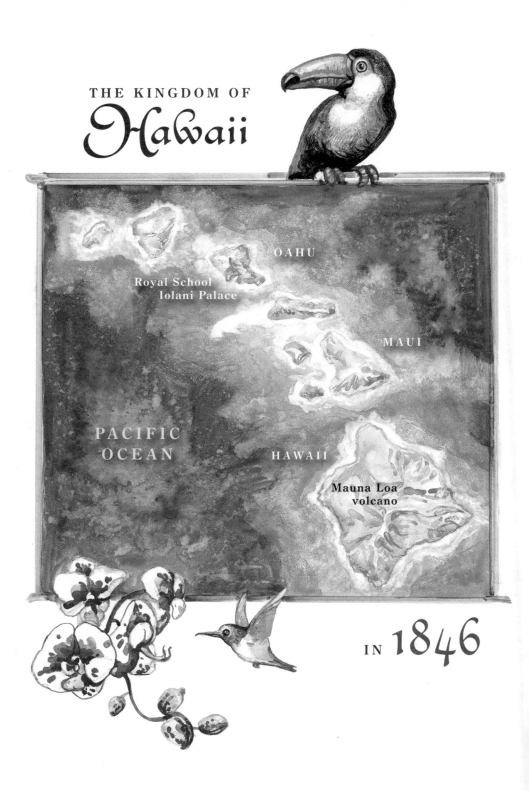

# THE KINGDOM OF
# Hawaii

OAHU

Royal School
Iolani Palace

MAUI

PACIFIC
OCEAN

HAWAII

Mauna Loa
volcano

IN 1846

The Hawaiian alphabet has twelve letters: a, e, h, i, k, l, m, n, o, p, u, and w. None of the letters are silent. Here is how to read some of the Hawaiian words in this book:

**aloha** (ah-LO-hah)—hello or goodbye

**Hawaii** (hah-WAE-ee)

**Kamehameha III** (kah-MAY-hah-MAY-hah)

**Kilauea** (kee-lah-WAY-ah)

**lei** (LAY-ee)—a flower necklace

**Liliuokalani** (lih-lee-uh-wah-kuh-LAH-nee)

**luau** (LU-ow)—a feast or party

**Mauna Loa** (MOW-noh LOH-wuh)

**Oahu** (oh-AH-hoo)

**Pele** (PAY-lay)—a volcano goddess

**poi** (PO-ee)—a thick soup

**tapa** (TAH-pah)—a type of cloth made from mulberry tree bark

# CHAPTER
## 1

## Lydia Goes to the Royal School

Seven-year-old Lydia and her best friend, Vicky, were excited. King **Kamehameha** and Lydia's father, Chief Paki, had come to their school today.

Their school was near the king's palace on the island of **Oahu** in the kingdom of **Hawaii**. It was called the Royal School because only royal children went there.

The king asked the class a question. "Do you all remember the awful thing that happened to our kingdom three years ago?"

"Yes," said Lydia's older brother, David. "It was 1843 when England overthrew our government."

The king nodded. "And on July 31, England's queen Victoria returned our government to us. Does anyone know what we call that day?"

Lydia raised her hand. "A happy day?" she suggested.

The king smiled. "It was a happy day, Liliu."

Liliu was Lydia's **Hawaiian** name. All the royal children had two names—one was **Hawaiian** and one was American.

"But we also call it Restoration Day," the king told her. "It's a day to be proud that we are not ruled by England, America, or any other nation that wants to change us."

"At the end of July, we will have a **luau** in honor of that happy day," Chief Paki told the class. "You are all invited."

After their talk, the king and Chief Paki stayed for a picnic outside. Mrs. Cooke served oatmeal, pie, vegetables, and bread. Mrs. Cooke and her husband were from America. They were teachers at the Royal School.

Lydia made a yucky face. She didn't like oatmeal. She would rather have **poi**. The king winked at her. Maybe he didn't like oatmeal either, she thought.

While Mrs. Cooke showed the children's schoolwork to the king and Chief Paki, the children played together.

"I want to give the king a present at the **luau**," Vicky told the others. "I'll make a **tapa** cloth out of mulberry tree bark."

"I'll carve a totem pole out of tiki wood for him," said David.

"That's a lot of work," said Bernice, Lydia's older sister. "Do you want me to help?"

"Sure," said David.

Lydia could not think of an idea for a gift at first. Then she looked at the garden. "I know! I'll make a **lei** for the king!"

She carefully wove a necklace of big red flowers. She tried it on.

Mrs. Cooke looked out the window. She frowned when she saw Lydia's necklace and called her over.

"Please take off that **lei**," she told her quietly.

"Why?" asked Lydia.

"Because flowers belong in the garden," said Mrs. Cooke.

Sometimes it seemed that her teacher didn't like anything **Hawaiian**, Lydia thought. Mrs. Cooke thought everyone should learn to do things the way Americans did. She gave them oatmeal instead of **poi** for lunch. And the royal children had to wear shoes to school. Most **Hawaiians** went barefoot.

Just then the king and Lydia's
father came back outside. She heard
them talking as they left the school.

"I built this school so the royal
children could learn to speak English
like the outsiders coming to our islands,"
the king said. "Because the children will
rule **Hawaii** someday, they must learn the
outsiders' ways. But sometimes I worry
they will forget the old ways of our people."

"I worry too," said Chief Paki. He and the king walked away.

As Lydia took off the necklace, she saw its flowers had turned a little brown. Flowers wouldn't last until the **luau**. She wanted to give the king a special gift that showed she loved **Hawaii**. It should be a gift that would last a long time. But what?

# CHAPTER 2

## Lydia and the Volcano

The next morning the students of the Royal School went on a field trip. Mrs. Cooke took them on a boat from **Oahu** to the Big Island of **Hawaii**. They were going to visit **Mauna Loa**. It was the largest volcano in the world.

Steam hissed from cracks in the volcano as Lydia and her classmates rode horses toward its top.

"The lava lake is up ahead," Lydia told Vicky. "Let's hurry and get there first."

"Yes!" said Vicky.

The girls soon reached the lava lake inside the **Kilauea** volcano on **Mauna Loa**. But they hadn't gotten there first.

A group of Americans were visiting the volcano too.

"**Aloha**!" Lydia and Vicky called to them.

"Hello!" they called back.

Lydia picked up a pretty lava rock. A rock was a gift that would last a long time.

"This rock is shaped just like a bear," she told Vicky. "Do you think it would make a good present to give the king at the **luau**?"

"No! It's bad luck to take the lava rocks, remember?" said Vicky.

Lydia sighed. "You're right. I don't want to give the king bad luck." She threw the rock into the lake. A stream of fire shot up where it landed.

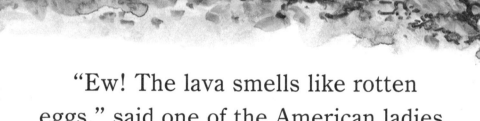

"Ew! The lava smells like rotten
eggs," said one of the American ladies.
She covered her nose.

One of the men pointed at something
on the ground by the edge of the lake.
"What's that?" he asked.

The lady looked closer and screamed.
"It's the head of a dead pig!"

"Don't be afraid," Lydia told her. "That is a present for **Pele**, the goddess of fire. Some people believe she lives in the volcano. They leave gifts for her, so the volcano will not erupt."

"Do you girls believe in **Pele**?" the American lady asked.

"No, our teacher taught us to pray to a Christian god," said Vicky.

"But sometimes we still give Pele gifts for good luck," said Lydia.

The lady smiled and pulled a coin out of her purse. She threw it into the lava.

"Now maybe I will have good luck!" she said.

# CHAPTER 3

## Lydia and the Songs

On the way back to school Mrs. Cooke gave Lydia a sheet of paper with a song written on it.

"Will you help everyone learn this hymn?" she asked.

Lydia nodded. "Yes, ma'am."

Children at the Royal School learned math, spelling, writing, and reading. But Lydia's favorite class was music. Bernice gave her lessons on the piano for an hour every day.

Lydia read the music notes on the sheet until she had learned the tune. When they got back to school she sang it aloud for the class.

They copied her. Soon the whole class had learned the hymn.

Vicky looked at the sheet music Lydia had read. "I wish I could read the notes as well as you," she said. "How do you do it?"

"I can't explain it," said Lydia. "To me, reading music is as easy as breathing."

After the song, Lydia's big brother, David, was angry. He wanted to go surfing in the ocean, but there was a new law against that.

"The Americans have decided surfing is too wild," he told the other children. "Now I can't ride my surfboard anymore."

"Why doesn't the king just tell the Americans to go away?" asked Lydia. "Then we could do what we want to."

"**Hawaii** is a small country. We aren't strong enough to make larger countries leave us alone," Bernice explained. "After all, England overthrew us just three years ago."

Everyone nodded.

"**Hawaii** is like a little fish that big fish want to gobble," said David.

Lydia saw how worried everyone was. She remembered that the king had been worried too. He wanted them to remember the old ways of **Hawaii**. Maybe she could help.

"Let's tell stories," she said.

"Okay," said Vicky. "That always makes us feel better."

Lydia began to tell the tale of **Hawaii**'s creation. She chanted the words in a singsong voice, which was the **Hawaiian** way of storytelling.

"When the stars were small eyes in the night," Lydia began.

"From the slime was the earth formed," Vicky continued.

"And the night gave birth to the starfish," Bernice added.

And the story went on. All of the children knew this and other stories by heart. The people of **Hawaii** told them over and over.

But the stories didn't make David feel better. He was still angry.

"Americans don't want us to surf or go barefoot," he said. "Maybe one day they will decide they don't like our songs either."

"Our mama taught the songs of **Hawaii** to us by singing them," said Bernice. "I want to sing them to my own children someday."

"I would be sad if Mrs. Cooke told us not to sing our songs," said Vicky. "Do you think we might forget them?"

That gave Lydia an idea. "Not if I can help it," she said.

# CHAPTER
4
### Lydia and the Luau

Finally the day of the big **luau** came. Lydia's parents were busy getting ready.

"Hundreds of guests are coming to the **luau** today," said Chief Paki. "But no one will go hungry. There will be two hundred seventy roasted pigs, five thousand fish, and more than two thousand coconuts at the **luau**!"

"Will there be **poi**, too?" asked Lydia.

"Don't worry," said her mama, Chiefess Konia. "Our servants cooked the roots of many taro plants to make plenty of **poi**."

Because they were royal children, Lydia and Vicky sat at the king's table during the **luau**. Other guests sat on mats on the ground around low tables.

After everyone had eaten, King **Kamehameha** stood. He began speaking in a loud voice so all the guests could hear.

"Today is Restoration Day!" he said.
"Let's all celebrate that **Hawaii** is still
an independent kingdom."

Everyone cheered and waved
**Hawaiian** flags.

After the king sat down again, Vicky gave him the **tapa** cloth she had made. Other people gave him gifts too. Then it was time for Lydia to give him her present.

She pulled out a roll of paper tied with a bow. Would the king like her gift?

King **Kamehameha** slowly unrolled the sheets of paper and read them.

"What's this, little Liliu?" he asked.

"It's some of the songs of **Hawaii**," she told him. "I wrote them for you, so none of us will ever forget them."

The king smiled a big smile. He liked her gift!

"What a wonderful idea," he told her. "No one has ever written these songs on paper before. I hope you will write more of them, so they will never be lost to us."

Lydia smiled back at the king. "I promise I will."

# CHAPTER 5

## Queen Lydia Liliuokalani

Lydia kept writing the words to old **Hawaiian** songs all of her life. She also made up new songs about **Hawaii**.

Years after the **luau**, her brother, David, was crowned king of **Hawaii**. After he died, Lydia became queen. By then the kingdom of **Hawaii** was in trouble. Many Americans wanted it to become part of the United States. Lydia and most **Hawaiian** people wanted it to stay an independent kingdom.

A group of Americans overthrew Lydia's kingdom in 1893. Five years later the United States took control of **Hawaii**.

Though she lost all of her power, Lydia never lost her love for **Hawaii**. She wrote a book about her life called *Hawaii's Story by Hawaii's Queen*.

# This time line lists the important events in Lydia Liliuokalani's life:

| | |
|---|---|
| 1838 | Lydia is born on September 2 to Chief Kapaakea and Chiefess Keohokalole. Chief Paki and Chiefess Konia adopt her. |
| 1842 | She begins school. |
| 1843 | England takes control of Hawaii, then gives it up. |
| 1862 | She marries an American named John Dominis. |
| 1874 | Her brother, David, becomes the king of Hawaii. He is known as King Kalakaua (kah-LAH-KAH-yoo-uh). |
| 1877 | David changes Lydia's name to Princess Liliuokalani. |
| 1878 | She writes her most famous Hawaiian song, "Aloha Oe." |
| 1887 | A group of Americans force King Kalakaua to let them make the laws. |
| 1887 | She meets Queen Victoria of England. |
| 1891 | King Kalakaua and his wife die. Lydia becomes queen of Hawaii. |
| 1893 | A group of Americans overthrows her kingdom. |
| 1895 | She is put on trial and imprisoned at her palace for eight months. |
| 1898 | The United States takes control of Hawaii. |
| | She writes a book about her life. |
| 1917 | She dies on November 11 at age 79. |
| 1959 | Hawaii becomes the fiftieth state in the United States. |
| 1993 | The U.S. government apologizes to native Hawaiians for the overthrow of the kingdom in 1893. |

# BEN 10 ALIEN FORCE™

# BEN'S KNIGHTMARE

SCHOLASTIC INC.

New York   Toronto   London   Auckland
Sydney   Mexico City   New Delhi   Hong Kong

ISBN-13: 978-0-545-16051-3
ISBN-10: 0-545-16051-0
TM & © 2009 Cartoon Network.
(s09)
Published by Scholastic Inc.
SCHOLASTIC and associated logos are trademarks and/or
registered trademarks of Scholastic Inc.

12 11 10 9 8 7 6 5 4 3 2          9 10 11 12 13 14/0

Illustrations by by Min Sung Ku and Hi-Fi Design
Printed in the U.S.A.
First printing, September 2009

"Good catch, Ship!"

Julie Yamamoto clapped as her pet jumped up and caught a Frisbee in his mouth.

Ben Tennyson shook his head. "It's hard to believe that Ship isn't from this planet," he said. "He's like a dog in so many ways."

"He's better than a dog," Julie replied. "No fleas!"

Kevin Levin pulled into the driveway in his bright green sports car.

"It's about time," said Ben's cousin, Gwen. "The movie's going to start soon."

Kevin climbed out of the car. "So we'll miss some lousy previews," he said. "I've got something much better to show you. Check this out."

Kevin held up a round metal device. "I got it at an underground alien tech swap. Isn't it awesome?"

"What is it?" Ben asked.

Kevin shrugged. "I don't know yet. I—hey!"

Before Kevin could finish, Ship jumped up and grabbed the device right out of his hand.

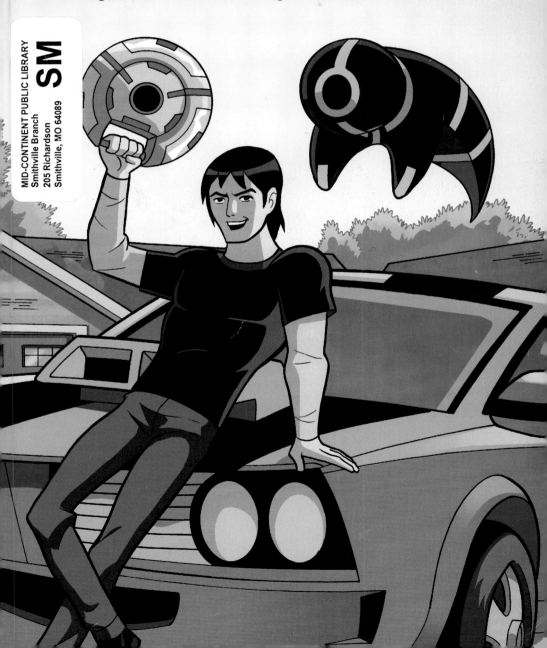

"Get back here, you crazy nano-mutt!"
Kevin yelled. He chased Ship across the yard.
Julie held up the Frisbee. "Here, Ship!" she
called out. "Let's trade!"

Ship ran toward Julie. Kevin dove after him, reaching out to grab the device.

*Zap!* The device accidentally went off. A green light shot out and hit Julie.

Julie's body glowed with green light. When the light faded, Julie looked . . . different. Her body was covered with green scales. Her hands looked like claws. Ben, Gwen, and Kevin gasped. "What's the matter?" Julie asked.

Gwen handed Julie a small mirror. "You'd better see for yourself."

"Okay, I'm lizard girl," Julie said, trying to stay cool. "There's got to be a reverse button, right?"

Kevin looked over the machine. "That would be a negative."

"I think I know what happened," said Kevin. "There was another device like this one at the swap. I bet that one is the reverse ray."

"So who got it?" Ben asked.

"The Forever Knights," Kevin replied. "No problem. We just break into their castle and steal it from them."

Ben groaned. The Forever Knights were a bunch of guys descended from the knights of old. Ben and his friends were on top of their enemies list.

"Stealing isn't the way to go," Ben said.

"What else can we do? Knock on the door and say 'pretty please'?" Kevin asked.

"All right," Ben said. "I'll go with Kevin."
"I'll hang with Julie," Gwen offered.
Ship jumped up and down.
"No way, Ship," Ben said. "I know you want to help. But you can't. The knights captured you once already."

Ben and Kevin drove through the woods to the Forever Knights' castle.

"I heard they beefed up security since the last time we were here," Kevin warned. "Breaking in could be tough."

"So what's the plan?" Ben asked. "Ring the bell and ask for a tour?"

"There's a small service door in the back," Kevin said. "It's usually not guarded."

They found the door—but it was locked shut.

"No problem," Ben said. He dialed up the Omnitrix and transformed into Goop. Then he slipped under the door and unlocked it.

"See how easy that was?" Kevin said. They stepped into a dark passageway.

Without warning, the floor opened up underneath their feet. It was a trap!

"*Whoaaaaaaaaaaaa!*" Ben and Kevin landed with a splash in a moat filled with black water.

Kevin felt something on his arm. He looked down to see a slimy tentacle. "Uh, Ben, I don't think we're alone."

A dozen tentacles splashed out of the water. Three of them wrapped around Kevin and started to drag him under.

Ben slapped the Omnitrix again. He transformed into another alien form—Big Chill. The blue, buglike alien grabbed Kevin and flew out of the water.

"Say freeze!" Big Chill hissed. He shot a blast of icy air at the moat. The water froze, trapping the tentacles in the ice.

"Let's keep moving," Kevin said.

They came to a door that led to another passageway. Kevin carefully took a step inside.

"No trapdoor," Kevin said. He put his other foot inside the passage . . .

. . . and triggered another booby trap. Sharp wood spears shot out of the wall.

"I got this one," Kevin said. He touched
the stone wall. A moment later, his whole
body had turned to stone.

Kevin charged through the passage, smashing the spears into splinters. Big Chill followed safely behind him until they reached the other side.

While Ben and Kevin made their way deeper into the castle, Julie was becoming more and more like a reptile. She pounced on a juicy moth.

"Maybe you should rethink that snack choice," Gwen advised. "I hear it's not easy to get rid of bug breath."

Kevin and Big Chill finally found their way to the weapons stash. The door was flanked by two stone gargoyle statues.

"Do you think the door is booby-trapped?" Big Chill asked.

"Could be," Kevin said. "I say we bust it down, grab the device, and get out of here."

Kevin raced toward the door, ready to knock it down.

Suddenly, the eyes of the gargoyles began to glow bright red. The stone creatures came to life. They pounced on Kevin.

"Of course," Big Chill said. "They're robots!"

Kevin somersaulted between the two gargoyles, dodging them. They turned on him, shooting red laser blasts from their eyes.

Bill Chill flew down the corridor and aimed a blast of freezing breath at the gargoyles.

The frozen robots shattered into pieces.
Big Chill quickly transformed back into Ben.
He opened the door to the weapons room.
"Let's make this fast," Ben said.

The room was loaded with alien tech. Kevin gave a low whistle. "Wow. What a stash."

"We're grabbing that lizard-reversing thing and getting out of here," Ben said. "No souvenirs, okay?"

"You are no fun sometimes," Kevin complained.

Kevin spotted the device on a shelf.
"Here it is," he said.
As soon as he grabbed the device, a
piercing alarm echoed through the castle.

"Run!" Ben cried.
They dashed back through the castle as fast as they could. Knights poured out of every doorway, chasing them.

Ben and Kevin raced outside, and a knight tackled Kevin. As he fell, Kevin tossed the device to Ben. But a knight knocked Ben out of the way. At that moment, Ship appeared out of nowhere! He leaped up and caught the device in his mouth.

Ben ran to the car. Behind him, Kevin had absorbed the knights' armor. Metal Kevin plowed through the knights, knocking them down. Then he jumped into the driver's seat.

"Thank goodness we got away," Ben sighed as they sped away. "What a *knight*-mare!"

The device worked perfectly. Soon Julie was back to normal.

"Thanks, guys," Julie said. "You know, I could really go for a bug—I mean, a burger."

Ben and Kevin gave Gwen a puzzled look.

Gwen just laughed. "You don't want to know!"